The Best Horse

by ELIZABETH VAN STEENWYK

SCHOLASTIC BOOK SERVICES

NEW YORK • TORONTO • LONDON • AUCKLAND • SYDNEY • TOKYO

To Dammy Williams Johnson,
who taught me all I know about barrel racing,
and to Bojangles,
who taught me all I know about horses.

ISBN: 0-590-03051-5

Copyright © 1977 by Elizabeth Van Steenwyk. All rights reserved. Published by Scholastic Book Services, a division of Scholastic Magazines, Inc.

12 11 10 9 8 7 6   0 1 2/8

Contents

Cover photo by Joan Farber

Frontispiece by Richard Amundsen

Janet's Announcement

Wendy shifted from one foot to the other, watching the school bus crawl slowly toward her like a giant yellow bug on the blacktop road. Her friend Janet, riding the bus, *had* to have some definite news today. Wendy couldn't bear waiting much longer.

It's Wednesday and Wednesday is definitely my best day, she thought. Good things *always* happen on Wednesdays. Like, I nearly always get a postcard from Aunt Sally on Wednesday from wherever she's traveling. So I just *know* Janet will tell me about the rodeo today.

As the bus gained speed coming over Blackberry Rise, Wendy tried not to think about Janet's news; it made her feel too anxious. Instead, she tried to guess what city Aunt Sally's card would be postmarked from this time — perhaps Bangkok, or Hong Kong, since she was traveling in the Orient. Maybe the spoon she sent would have a dragon on the handle. Aunt Sally always sent her a spoon from every country she visited. So far, Wendy had twenty-one silver spoons.

Someday, Wendy thought, I'm going to travel too, like Aunt Sally. But I'll always come back to Colorado, no matter how far I roam. She looked around at the rolling flatlands, lush and green now with ripening sugar beets. Yes, she'd always come back to Logan County. This was her home.

Kim Marshall ran across the road to the bus stop.

"I was afraid I'd missed the bus," she panted. "Have you got a comb and mirror, Wendy?"

Wendy shook her head no.

"Oh, good grief, what am I going to do? My hair is such a mess!" Kim bent over a puddle of rain water. She turned this way and that, trying to catch her reflection.

Kim sure has gotten stuck on herself all of a sudden, Wendy thought, watching her. Always fixing her hair! She must like some boy and she's trying to impress him.

Wendy sighed and looked away. She just knew no decent boy would look at her. Her long blonde hair was straight as cornstalks and her eyes were green — algae green. As for her turned-up nose . . . oh well, she really didn't care, anyway. All that *really* mattered was riding her horse Kickapoo.

The school bus rolled to a stop. Glancing up at the row of windows, Wendy spied Janet's eager face. Her friend looked about ready to leap through the glass. She knows, Wendy thought. She knows!

Wendy quickly climbed the steps of the bus. She barely said hello to Mr. Mooney, the driver, and rushed down the aisle. Janet moved over and Wendy slid in beside her.

"Wendy! Guess what!" Janet's eyes were dancing, and her high-pitched voice carried through the din of thirty other voices.

"Well, what?" Wendy demanded. "Come on, Janet, tell me! You know I'm dying to hear."

"Okay, okay. Well, Dad came home from the Farm Club meeting last night and said — said that the members have voted to sponsor the Little Britches Rodeo in August! Isn't that great?" Janet talked so fast her words ran together.

Wendy felt shivers down her spine. At last her dream had become real enough to talk about at home. Little Britches Rodeo was coming to Sterling, and she would ride in it; she would finally become a barrel racer!

"I can't believe it," she said. "Pinch me so that I'll know I'm really hearing this."

Just then, someone did. Pinched her right on her neck.

"Ouch!" She jumped and swung around — and looked straight into the freckled face of Beaver Wolcott. He grinned, showing all his braces.

"Hi. You said pinch me, so I did." He grinned again, then suddenly pretended to read his math book — upside down.

Wendy raised her arm, then caught sight of Mr. Mooney, the driver, looking at them in the rear view mirror. She dropped her arm. She could get even with Beaver later. "Boys," she muttered. "They can be so dumb when they're only eleven." She herself was twelve. Had been for a month now, and it really made a difference. She really felt older.

"Why didn't you call me last night, as soon as you found out about Little Britches?" Wendy asked Janet.

"Mom said it was too late. Besides, I hadn't finished my homework." Janet dipped into her lunch box, unwrapped a cupcake, and bit into it.

Maybe it was just as well I didn't know last night, Wendy thought, as they bounced through the outskirts of Sterling. I would probably have blurted the

4

news right out to Mom, and then we would have had a fight about it. This way, I've got all day to figure out what to say.

A sweater sailed through the air and landed on the seat beside Wendy. She turned and saw Heidi Buckler waving at her and holding up her history book.

Probably wants to copy my homework again, Wendy thought, as she tossed the sweater back. She shrugged her shoulders at Heidi and turned back to Janet.

"How many events are you going to enter in the rodeo?" Janet asked, through a spray of crumbs. "I think I'll enter all of them for junior girls."

"All of them?" Wendy asked. "That's expensive. There's an entry fee for every one, you know."

"Oh, my dad will pay for them," Janet said. "No sweat."

Janet didn't know how lucky she was, Wendy thought, with parents who would pay for her entry fees as well as the other costs that went along with entering a rodeo. Her own Mom said they couldn't afford it. Wendy knew that money had been scarce since Dad died, a couple of years ago. Mom was having a tough time running the farm with the help of just Lockjaw, the hired man. But it was more than that. There was something bothering her that

Wendy couldn't understand. Mom had said flat out one day that Wendy couldn't be a participant in Little Britches, even if it were sponsored right here in Sterling. Even if it were free.

"What events are *you* going to enter?" Janet asked.

Wendy shook herself loose from her tangled rope of thoughts. "Oh, just one event, just barrel racing. That's all I've ever wanted to do."

"You'll be good at that." Janet pushed back her short brown hair. "The way you can ride Kickapoo."

Kickapoo. Good old Kickapoo, Wendy thought. An eight-year-old sorrel gelding, with one white stocking, he stood fourteen hands high. He had good withers to keep a saddle in place and hocks set well under him for a quick getaway. He was perfect for barrel racing. Yes, she could win on Kickapoo — if she could convince Mom to let her enter the rodeo.

Wendy saw herself in the arena. It was opening day and she sat astride Kickapoo dressed in jeans and matching vest with glittery stuff on them. Then the crowd roared as she raced Kick around those barrels (55-gallon oil drums). The gelding's muscles quivered against her legs as she held the reins lightly to guide him through the cloverleaf pattern. Then, with one final spurt, she and Kickapoo galloped

6

madly back to the starting line, breaking the all-time world record. Oh, wow, she thought, shuddering with pleasure.

Wendy waited until most of the kids had pushed and shoved their way down the aisle and out the door. This will be a summer that's different, she thought. In just a few days now, I'll say good-bye to sixth grade and Simpson Elementary forever. It's junior high in the fall. Going to junior high would be kind of neat, but first came the rodeo in August. And I will be in it, she promised herself. Even if Mom said no, I'll enter anyway. No one will keep me from becoming a barrel racer.

Kickapoo

"How's my favorite railbird tonight?" A familiar deep voice rumbled behind her.

Wendy hadn't heard Lockjaw approach as she sat on the rail fence that wound around the barnyard. She'd been busy with her own thoughts and plans, watching Kickapoo mosey around, cropping tufts of grass as he cooled down after their workout. For several weeks now, she'd been conditioning him, strengthening his muscles and building his wind for the barrel race.

Now she turned and looked into the familiar weather-tanned face. "Evening, Lockjaw."

"What are you ponderin' up there on your perch?" he asked, leaning against the gatepost. "Some boy you got your eye on at school?"

"Oh, Lockjaw," she laughed. "You know I hate boys."

He laughed, too, a long, low rumble. "That won't always be the case."

Wendy wondered if she should tell him what she was thinking about. She'd need his help to carry through her plan of entering the rodeo. Nobody was more of an expert on rodeos than Lockjaw Livingston, ex-bronc riding champ of Colorado and later, one of the bravest clowns of all time.

"I need three barrels," she said.

"Aha." The sound told her he understood what she meant. Now she had to convince him.

"Lockjaw?"

"Yes, Wendy?"

"I've got to learn to barrel race and you've got to help me."

"Now pull in your reins, little girl," Lockjaw said. He pushed his Stetson back from his forehead. "You know your Mama is against this. I don't want to get caught in the middle of a family disgruntlement."

"But you're the *same* as family, Lockjaw," she said. "You and Dad were like brothers on the rodeo trail, you said. And the way you've worked this farm, it's just like it was your own. Mom's said time and again, there wouldn't be a farm today, without you."

"That's pleasurable to hear, Wendy, but I'm not your blood kin, so I don't see how I can vote on this."

Wendy looked off toward the rosy horizon. "Lockjaw," she asked finally, in a puzzled tone, "do you know why Mom's so dead set against me entering Little Britches?"

"I think you'd best ask her, little railbird," he said softly. Then he headed for the barn.

Wendy watched him go. His limp was hardly noticeable tonight. That's because the weather's nicer now, she thought. He said that when the days got warmer, his leg got looser. That was his way of saying his leg didn't hurt so much then.

He'd been badly hurt in the rodeo. He said once, when the pain in his leg was bad, that he'd figured they might as well collect his bones and throw them to the winds.

Was it because of Lockjaw's accident that Mom didn't want her to barrel race? Did Mom think she might get hurt? But the barrel race wasn't dangerous, no more than riding a bike. It wasn't anything like the bronc riding that Lockjaw and Dad had done, nor the clowning to divert the wild-eyed broncs and bulls from the riders they'd just thrown. Clowning was the most dangerous part of all. That was what had nearly killed Lockjaw.

It was time she asked Mom straight out.

Wendy heard the screen door squeak even before she heard Mom's voice. "Come to supper, you two."

Wendy turned and waved. "I'll be right there, soon's I bed down Kickapoo."

"Five minutes, then," Mom said. The screen door squeaked again and slammed shut. Wendy hopped down from the rail and whistled. Kickapoo looked up, his ears pricked forward. Slowly he ambled toward her.

"Come on, fella," she said, heading for the barn. He nickered softly. In the fading sunset, his reddish brown coat took on a velvety rippling sheen. Wendy suddenly felt that she loved Kickapoo better than anything in the world, and to tell him so, she rubbed her face on his. It smelled faintly of hay and sun and dust.

"Oh, Kickapoo, you do understand, don't you?"

Blinking his dark brown eyes at her, he blew air through his nostrils, and then his shoes clopped softly on the dirt as they walked to the barn.

"Mom called," Wendy said to Lockjaw's dim outline in the cow stall.

"Be right there," he said.

Wendy opened the gate to Kickapoo's stall and saw that Lockjaw had already filled the bin with hay. Kickapoo attended to it immediately, crunching with his strong jaws. Wendy brushed him down, then threw her brushes and comb in the tack box.

"He ought to be in pasture now, this time of year," Lockjaw said.

Wendy knew that, but she hated to give up her nightly ritual with Kickapoo. It was the best time of day. "Tomorrow," she said. "Maybe tomorrow I'll turn him out."

Mom was dishing up the vegetables as she and Lockjaw entered the warm kitchen. They washed at the sink and then sat down.

"Where's Aunt Sally's card from this time?" Mom asked.

"Hong Kong."

Lockjaw helped himself to mashed potatoes and carrots. "Sure gits around, don't she."

"She lives such a wonderful life," Mom said.

Wendy looked up at Mom. The sharp lines on her face had softened to a dreamy, faraway look. Wendy thought, it's funny, but Mom never seems to be jealous of Aunt Sally's life. She just acts as though she's there, right with Aunt Sally, enjoying all those places that she can never really know. There was a big word they'd studied in English that said it right, she remembered, but she couldn't think of it now. Something like sympathy, only it had a different beginning.

"Mom . . ." Wendy started to ask the question that had been nagging at her.

"Oh, Wendy, I almost forgot," Mom began quickly. "I heard from Sally today, too. She wrote me a letter."

"What did she say?"

"Well, not much, except that she did enclose a check for your lessons."

Wendy swallowed some biscuit. "Lessons? What lessons?" she asked.

"Well, I had mentioned to her once that I thought you should take some dancing lessons this summer, before you entered junior high."

"Dancing lessons? Oh, Mom!"

"Now you hear me out, Wendy." Mom looked at her and their eyes met. "Your Aunt Sally is just as concerned about your future as I am. That's why she sent this check as sort of a belated birthday present, in addition to those pretty clothes. She has felt, as I do, that out here in the country you miss out on certain . . . well, certain refinements. They're going to be important to you when you go on to high school and maybe college and then marry some nice young man with a good future."

"I'm not going to take any dumb dancing lessons."

"Wendy." Mom's voice had a wheedling sound to it. "After Aunt Sally has agreed to pay for them?"

"How could she agree to pay for something I didn't agree to take? I don't want to do anything this summer but work with Kickapoo and enter the rodeo in August." There. She'd said it. This time *said* it, not asked it.

"I thought we had that settled." Mom's voice had a warning edge to it.

Lockjaw cleared his throat. "Maybe," he said, uneasily, "maybe I ought to see about the chickens."

"No, Lockjaw," Mom said. "Please don't leave. I'm sorry we've made you feel uncomfortable."

Wendy knew that was meant for her. A direct hit.

14

Pow. She was supposed to be a good girl, not disturb anyone, do what she was told. But why couldn't she enter Little Britches? Out here in the West everyone rode, everyone went to rodeos. Why couldn't she?

"Mom, why do you hate rodeos so much?"

"How can you ask that, Wendy? Your father traveled the circuit for I don't know how many summers. And here sits Lockjaw, one of the best . . ." Her voice trailed off while Wendy watched her swallow hard and push food around on her plate.

"Wendy, it's hard for me to put into words — all the things I want for you. I can't just say them right out to you now, here at the supper table. But I know what I *don't* want. I *don't* want you to take up with rodeo ways."

Wendy traced her fork back and forth on the orange squares in the plastic tablecloth. She felt her feelings swelling up, about to boil over. She had to leave before that happened. She stood up so suddenly, her chair fell back.

"Can I be excused?"

"But you haven't finished your supper. And there's dessert . . ."

"I don't want any dessert. I don't want any dancing lessons. I don't want *anything*." Wendy ran from the kitchen and out into the soft night. Heading for the barn and Kickapoo, she felt her eyes smart with tears. Why did life suddenly have to get so complicated and rotten?

The Palomino Arrives

"Let's try it one more time, Kickapoo," Wendy said.

She mopped her face with a damp kerchief and settled her wide-brimmed hat more firmly on her head. It sure was hot with that sun beating down, she thought.

Slowly she eased Kickapoo into the routine again. She'd been working him for the past hour, starting out at a walk, training him to turn and pivot short. He must eventually do this at a gallop, but now, even at the much slower pace, it wasn't going right.

She eased him near the fence, then entered the pattern she'd set up. Was it her teaching, she wondered. She was a good rider, she knew that, and she'd watched the older girls barrel race at fairs and rodeos for as long as she could remember. No, she knew what she had to do and what her horse had to do. Only trouble was, Kickapoo didn't seem interested in barrel racing. She frowned, trying not to be anxious.

Lockjaw had watched her the last few days and, although he vowed to stay out of her quarrel with Mom, she knew it was more than his rodeo-loving heart could stand, not to help her get ready. A day or so ago, while he was milking the cow, he'd said, knowing Wendy was nearby, "Molly, if you want to barrel race you got to shorten your stirrups more." And last night he'd told Hector, the battered old calico cat who always hung around the barn, "Hector, you got to remember to git that horse's hocks under him so he'll brake on the pivot. That'll cut seconds off your time in the barrel race."

Wendy had grinned in spite of her anxiety. The picture of Hector atop Kickapoo, digging for home in the rodeo arena, was so funny she'd almost laughed out loud.

"Hey, Wendy!" A girl's voice called to her from the front gate. It was Janet. Now she came riding her Appaloosa down the tree-shaded lane toward the barnyard.

Wendy halted Kickapoo in a small patch of shade from the tack shed roof, and looked up, admiring Janet's easy command of her horse. She really sits neat, she thought.

"How's everything going?" Janet asked. She reined in her Appaloosa near Wendy.

"Oh, I don't know!" Wendy sounded discouraged, even to herself. "We just can't work together this morning."

"I noticed you were having some trouble." Janet stroked her horse as he stomped and eyed Kickapoo nervously. "Hold still, Hoofer."

"I can't get him to roll out." Wendy pushed her hat back.

"Maybe everything will go better when you get your barrels," Janet said. "You *are* going to get some barrels pretty soon, aren't you?"

"Sure. Any day now." Wendy felt Janet's eyes glued on her. "Oh, Janet, I just don't know."

"You mean you and your Mom are still fighting about this? It's been two weeks now."

"Yeah. She says no barrel racing. Just dancing lessons."

"Dancing lessons aren't going to be all that bad."

"You're going to take them?" Wendy couldn't believe it.

"Yeah, from Mrs. Twillabee, in town."

That must be the same teacher Mom wants me to take lessons from, thought Wendy. "How are you going to have time to practice for the rodeo if you're in town learning how to dance with some boy?" she asked.

"I've decided not to enter the goat-tail tying or the trail course. So that just leaves barrel racing, breakaway calf-roping, and pole bending." Janet ticked them off on her fingers. "I can work on them easy because that's all I've got to do."

That's right, Wendy thought. Janet didn't have special chores during the summer as she did. *She* had to work in the vegetable garden, and she always took over the full care of the chickens during the summer. That freed Lockjaw to concentrate on the pay crop of sugar beets, and Mom could get all her canning done. Actually, Wendy wouldn't have much time left over for dancing lessons, with all her chores, and training Kick for the barrel race besides.

"How are you going to pay for entering the rodeo, if your Mom won't help you?" Janet asked. "Besides the entry fee, there's the hauling fee and riding clothes. And your Mom has to sign the medical statement. Don't forget that."

"I've got it all worked out in my head," Wendy said.

"That's a lot of money," Janet insisted. "Probably twenty-five dollars."

"Do you think I don't know that?"

"Where you gonna get it? You told me you don't get much of an allowance. You'd have to save for thirty years. . . ."

They looked up as a truck and horse trailer pulled into the lane. "Wonder who that is?" Wendy said, hoping to distract Janet.

"Maybe you could make a deal with your Mom," Janet continued. "Take dancing lessons if she'll give you rodeo money."

Wendy looked at her and wondered if Janet could see inside her head. She'd had that in mind for a few days now, and if that didn't work, then she'd switch to her emergency plan. Knowing Mom the way she did, though, she knew it would be pretty hard to make any deals about anything.

The truck and trailer halted in the driveway near them. Dust stirred up by the truck settled into a fine film over everything.

Wendy licked her dry lips clean as she dismounted. Tying Kickapoo to the fence, she saw Lockjaw hurrying from the barn and heard the screen door squeak as Mom came out to stand on the porch.

"Morning, Wendy, Mrs. Herstead." Doc Galloway climbed down from the truck, took off his Stetson and wiped his forehead. He was an old rodeo friend of Lockjaw's from over Greeley way.

"Doc, my old friend." Lockjaw hurried up to pump Doc's hand. "You're really gonna do it this time."

"Yep, it's finally for real. I won't be back for six months, if then. Maybe I'll git me a job in the movies and never come back." Doc slapped his Stetson on his thigh as he shook with laughter.

"Have a good time in California with your daughter," Mom called and waved before she went back in the house.

Wendy remembered now, hearing about Doc going on a long visit to see his kids in California. He'd sold his land and most of the stock.

"I sold most everything but my old sidekick here," Doc said. "I'm just not ready to sell my best friend yet."

Together the men worked to back the aging Palomino mare out of the trailer.

"Just can't sell my friend, Buckwheat," Doc repeated. Wendy heard the catch in his voice. Old Doc feels the same about his horse as I do about Kickapoo, she thought.

"She can pasture with Kickapoo as long as you want," Lockjaw said. "By the time you come back, she won't even remember you."

"You're probably right at that," Doc laughed. "She'll be so fat and sassy, I won't be able to ride her for sure." He paused, then seemed to have a sudden thought. "Say, Wendy, any time you want to ride Buckwheat, just go right ahead. She'll need the exercise, for sure."

Wendy looked at the Palomino. Ride that old nag, she thought, when I could be on Kickapoo? Buckwheat was dull-colored compared with Kick, and she sagged with age.

"Thanks, Mr. Galloway," Wendy said and walked over to Janet. The two men led the animal to the pasture gate, talking and laughing as they went.

"Can't you just see me on Buckwheat in the rodeo?" Wendy said. She looked at Kickapoo's sleek coat, his fine conformation. He'd be so gorgeous, she thought, whipping around the barrels in the cloverleaf pattern, then digging for home with his mane and tail flying. His feet will hardly touch the ground, he'll be so fast and light.

"She's about had it," Janet agreed. She turned Hoofer around. "I have to go. I promised I'd be home for lunch on time, and then I have to wash my hair for dancing class this afternoon. It's the first session."

"Who else is going?" Wendy asked.

"Oh, Kim, Heidi, Beaver. . . . "

"Practically everybody."

"Yeah, we're all going to suffer together," Janet laughed.

Maybe, Wendy thought, maybe it won't be too bad if my friends are there. And maybe Mom won't be too unreasonable if I give in first. Maybe she will trade off the dancing for some barrels. Just the barrels. It might work. Anyway, it's worth a try.

The screen door squeaked. "Wendy," Mom called. "Run out and ask Doc to stay for lunch."

"Okay."

"You're welcome too, Janet," Mom said.

24

"Thanks, Mrs. Herstead, but I have to get along home."

The screen door squeaked again.

Janet sat looking at the house. "Sure don't understand about your Mom," she began. "You'd think she'd want you to barrel race too."

"Too? What do you mean?"

"Her being the champion and all."

"My Mom?" Wendy's voice shot upward. "My Mom was a barrel racer?"

"That's what my Mom said last night. Back when they were in high school, they both rode. Guess nobody could beat your Mom and she went on to compete in the big time. That's how she met your Dad."

Wendy leaned against the fence for support. If Janet had told her she had purple hair, Wendy couldn't have been more surprised.

Janet leaned over and looked at her closely. "Wendy," she said softly. "Didn't you know that?"

Wendy licked her lips which suddenly felt dry, and shook her head silently.

Janet started to say something, then changed her mind. Instead, she clicked Hoofer around and loped down the lane. The sunlight filtered unevenly through the trees on Janet and Hoofer as they hurried along.

Kickapoo nudged her shoulder and Wendy turned to him. "Come on, Kick, it's too hot to work any more." She untied him and led him to the pasture gate. "I've got to get inside. Mom's got some explaining to do."

Mom Agrees If . . .

Wendy stood at her bedroom window and watched as Doc said good-bye to Lockjaw. The two men thumped each other on the back, shook hands a couple of times, and drew lines in the dirt with the toes of their boots as they talked. Finally, Doc climbed into the cab of his truck. He circled the driveway and drove off down the lane. Lockjaw watched him leave, then turned back toward the barn. Wendy heard the screen door squeak, so she knew Mom must have been watching, too. Now, maybe, she'd come upstairs and they could talk. And none too soon, Wendy thought angrily.

There hadn't been time to talk before lunch. The

chickens had started squawking just as Janet left, so Wendy had hurried to see what the ruckus was about. She suspected it was Hector lurking around the henhouse again, playing his silly game of stalking the setting hens. He had so many pecks on his ears from those chickens, you'd think he'd learn, she thought, but he still insisted on doing his lion act about once a week. Wendy couldn't find him, so she calmed the hens and went into the house. By that time, Lockjaw and Doc were there, washing up at the kitchen sink, so Wendy could only glare angrily at Mom and say, "What horse did you barrel race on?"

Mom looked up, startled, her hands frozen midway between the hot biscuits and raspberry jam. Neither spoke during the rest of the meal, but let the comfortable hum of conversation between Lockjaw and Doc fill the air that hung heavy between them.

Now Wendy lay on her bed and opened the box containing her spoon collection. One by one, she took them out and placed them in two neat rows across her pink bedspread. Some of the spoons were plain silver, some had enameled handles with scenes of faraway places engraved on them. All of them were valuable and fun to look at. She could pick up a spoon and imagine she was in Holland, surrounded by blue windmills, or in London, looking at the silvery Parliament buildings. She could travel around the world, herself, just by looking at her spoons. Next to Kickapoo, she thought, I love my spoons best. She wondered how much money they would be worth if she had to put her emergency plan in motion. Then she thought, I don't want to think about that. It makes me feel so terrible.

Wendy heard a light tap on the door. "Come in." Quickly she put her feet on the floor. Mom hated shoes on the bedspread.

Mom entered, carrying several large, leatherbound scrapbooks in her arms. She placed them on the bed before Wendy.

"I really meant to tell you long before this," Mom said. "I didn't want you to find out from someone else. I'm truly sorry."

Wendy looked at Mom, all her anger suddenly gone. Sometimes grownups confused Wendy more than her math lessons. Just when she thought she had them figured out, with all the pluses and minuses and x's for unknowns in the right columns, they did something to upset her figuring.

Like now. Like Mom saying she was sorry.

"What's this?" Wendy poked at the scrapbooks.

"Back in the days when I was proud of my rodeo riding, I used to collect newspaper clippings and pictures about it," Mom said. "I can't imagine why I haven't thrown them away long ago."

Wendy wanted to open the scrapbooks, which smelled musty like the attic, and look inside. She wanted to see this other person who was also her mother, and whom she hadn't known existed until an hour or so ago. She traced her fingers on the design embossed on the leather. Oh, how she wanted to turn those pages! But she hesitated, waiting for an invitation. It wasn't right until she was invited.

"Yes, I really had meant to tell you long before this," Mom was saying. She fussed with the ruffled white curtains. "But I couldn't. You see, I thought that if you knew, then there'd be no way I could stop you." She turned to look at Wendy. "I knew you'd say, if you were in the rodeo once, why can't I be?" Mom smiled and Wendy smiled back. Mom knew her all right.

"Well, why *can't* I be?" Wendy asked. "What's so wrong with the rodeo?"

"Look at me." Mom's voice sounded sad. "The

rodeo led me here to this farm, where I'll stay for the rest of my life."

"What's the matter with the farm?" Wendy asked. She couldn't imagine living anywhere else. It was home.

"Someday you'll understand what I mean."

Why do grownups always say that, Wendy thought.

"It's not this farm, exactly," Mom began. "It's just that I want more for you. I want you to see the world, to go to exciting places, do exciting things." She paused, and picked up one of the spoons. Then she said, almost fiercely, "I want the world to be more for you than just a scene on the handle of a spoon!"

Wendy saw that Mom had the same wistful look on her face she wore when she talked about Aunt Sally. Only this time, Mom hadn't mentioned Aunt Sally. Can you talk about a person and not say her name, Wendy wondered.

"Did Aunt Sally ever ride in the rodeo?"

"Oh, no." Mom's answer was quick. "She was too delicate for that sort of life."

Wendy had never thought of Aunt Sally as delicate. How could anyone be delicate with fingernails that long and sharp? No, she'd never really thought of Aunt Sally in any way at all except, maybe, lucky for being so rich and getting to do whatever she wanted.

"Mom," Wendy said. "Please, just this once, let me barrel race."

Mom looked at her a long time, as if she were measuring her daughter. "It's really important to you, isn't it?" she said at last.

"Oh, yes!"

"Wendy, I've been so against this, it's almost impossible for me to say yes."

Wendy sensed victory. Mom didn't sound nearly so positive now. "Just this once, please. I promise I'll do all my chores without being told. I'll go to dancing class without complaining." Oh, how she hated to say that. "I'll even pay all the rodeo fees, if you'll just get me the barrels. They don't cost too much, do they?"

"No. Lockjaw might even know someone who's got some barrels just sitting around, that we could get free." Suddenly Mom turned and looked at her. "Wendy, how are you going to pay the money to enter the rodeo?"

Wendy swallowed hard and busied herself with the spoons, carefully wrapping each one in its tissue paper. She'd never told Mom anything but the exact truth before.

"Oh," she began. "I've been saving my allowance and most of my Christmas money that Aunt Sally sent me."

She hoped that Mom wouldn't do any sudden calculations about money she'd blown at the 4-H Fair last spring, or at the Sunday School picnic game booths on Memorial Day. And nearly every Saturday, when they went to town to buy groceries, Wendy couldn't resist wandering in the stores.

"I need to think a little more," Mom said. "I'll decide by supper time tonight." She stood up.

"If I say yes, I'll ask Lockjaw to find three barrels for you, but you'll have to pay for the rest." Mom sounded firm. "I'm glad you have been saving," she continued. "I really don't have a cent to spare right now. A couple of irrigation pipes have to be replaced and I simply can't squeeze one more cent out of the budget. I'll even need the egg money for groceries this month."

Wendy's spirits began to bubble. I know Mom's already decided it's yes, she thought. I'll finally get to ride Kickapoo in the rodeo.

She started to drift away into her favorite daydream, when Mom's voice brought her back into sharp focus.

"Listen, what's bothering the chickens?"

"That Hector," Wendy said. "I tried to catch him before lunch."

Mom looked out the window. "Is that when you left the gate open to the chicken yard?"

Wendy looked, too. The gate was partially obscured by the elm tree, now in full leaf. That's why no one had noticed the open gate until now, when the chickens discovered an escape from Hector. The chickens were strutting all over the backyard, some had even started down the lane. Wendy knew if they got out onto the road, she could lose half the flock.

She turned and ran for the stairs. How awful, she thought. Just when I'm about to have something go my way, I nearly ruin it. I hope this doesn't upset Mom so much that she'll say no, just when she was about to say yes!

Barrel Race Practice

Three days later, Lockjaw drove up the lane with three 55-gallon oil drums bouncing in the bed of the pickup. Wendy raced out of the chicken yard, barely remembering to fasten the gate, and reached the pasture just as Lockjaw pulled into it.

"Where do you want 'em?" he asked, climbing out of the pickup.

"Let's see." Wendy felt overwhelmed. "Where's the best place?"

"That level spot right over there looks good to me," Lockjaw pointed out.

"That's great, that's perfect," Wendy said.

As Lockjaw unfastened the gate of the pickup and hopped up on the back, Wendy whistled to Kickapoo, who was grazing in a far corner of the pasture. He looked up, but at the sight of the truck he seemed reluctant to come. Buckwheat, grazing nearby, nickered as if in answer, then came at a lope. She sure is light on her feet, Wendy thought, for being such an old girl.

Lockjaw rolled the barrels off the truck and together they stationed them on the level ground.

"What do you think, Lockjaw?" Wendy asked, trying to measure the distance between the barrels. "Is this about it?"

Lockjaw took off his Stetson and scratched his gray head. "Lemme see, now. You ride in the clover leaf pattern, right?"

"Yes, but it looks like a triangle, the way you lay out the barrels," Wendy said. "The base barrels in the triangle are thirty yards apart and the single barrel is thirty-five yards from the base barrels."

"You been studyin' on this for awhile, haven't you, Wendy?"

"I could have told you in my sleep," she grinned.

"Then tell me what you got to do when you git on your horse."

"Is this exam time?" She tried to sound stern but couldn't bring it off. Her smile wouldn't go away.

"It's a good idea to have your moves planned out." Lockjaw looked as happy as she felt.

Wendy thought a moment. "When I begin, I'll take the right barrel first — go round it turning to the right," she said. "Then I'll turn left around the second barrel. Then I'll go to the top of the triangle and turn left around that barrel before I run for home."

"What's Kickapoo's best lead?"

"His left lead is his favorite."

"Then you got your work cut out for you, Wendy," Lockjaw said. "He has to lead right to turn right."

"Lockjaw," Wendy began. "Does he really have to use his right lead on the right turn? Kickapoo is so stubborn sometimes — about changing, I mean."

"He won't be in proper balance if you don't make him do it like I said," Lockjaw reminded her. "You know that as well as I do. Wendy, you got to be the boss of that horse, remember that."

"When should he change to his left lead?"

"We'll work it out after you saddle up."

Wendy led Kickapoo to the barn and threw his saddle pad over his back. Then she stationed the saddle, slightly above his withers. Next she fastened

37

the cinch under his belly and walked him up and down the length of the barn. Then she checked his cinch again. Sure enough, it was loose.

"You like to play tricks, don't you, Kickapoo?" she said. "Bloating out your belly is your favorite so I won't cinch you too tight." She led him back to his stall and tightened the cinch, then reached for the bridle. After removing his halter, she placed the snaffle bit between his teeth as she pulled the bridle up over his nose. Then she pulled his ears through, tossed the reins over and onto the saddle horn, shortened the stirrups slightly, and mounted him.

They walked to the barn door and Wendy looked over at the pasture at her gorgeous, beautiful barrels. "This is where we start work, Kick. We've only got five weeks, so let's get moving."

She trotted him around the pasture for awhile, letting him warm up. Finally, she stretched him out into a long stride; they followed the fence line all the way around, and returned to the barrels in a nice, easy lope. Then Wendy felt he was ready.

They approached a barrel and Kickapoo eyed it warily. "It's just an oil drum," she said. "Now come on." Suddenly Buckwheat appeared beside her, trotting alongside, turning when Kickapoo turned. "Go away, Buckwheat." Wendy slapped at the Palomino with her hand.

Lockjaw hurried up and grabbed Buckwheat's halter. "Looks like Buckwheat wants to study on barrel racing, too," he said, leading her away.

Wendy began to walk Kickapoo toward the barrel.

"Lean into him, Wendy," Lockjaw called from the fence. "Ride up on him, apply pressure at his girth with your inside leg so he'll get the idea he's got to turn his body."

Wendy followed Lockjaw's instructions and Kickapoo responded.

"Now lead his nose to the right with your right hand rein," Lockjaw continued.

Wendy and Kickapoo circled the first barrel and headed for the next one.

"Check him, Wendy," Lockjaw called. Wendy followed his instructions, then waited for Kickapoo to gather himself for the change in lead.

Wendy sat down hard going around the second barrel to the left, then half rose from the saddle as she urged him to the third one. Once again, she sat down hard so that he'd tuck his back legs under; she squeezed near the girth with her inside leg, and near his flank with her outside leg.

"Now, let him go," Lockjaw called excitedly. "Let him run against the bridle and dig for home."

Wendy let it all out, urging Kickapoo toward an imaginary line some distance away from the barrels. She knew the distance had to be about sixty feet away according to the rules, and she tried to guess at it as Kickapoo cut loose.

"That was real good," Lockjaw called. "I think he's got the idea."

Wendy was bursting with happiness. Kickapoo enjoys this as much as I do, she thought.

"I'm going to work him some more," she said, stopping by the fence. "I'll pretend this is home base and see how fast I can bring him out."

"Not too fast, Wendy," Lockjaw said, making himself comfortable on the top railing. "Remember, you have to walk him first, then trot him, before he starts to lope through his paces. Gallopin' comes last of all."

Wendy turned Kickapoo and urged him toward the barrel once more, insisting on his right lead. Just as they reached the barrel, Kickapoo stopped. "Come on Kick," she said. "Move!"

He shook his mane and backed off. Wendy dug him slightly with her heels, to let him know she meant business. But Kickapoo snorted and shook himself, and backed off again.

"Be the boss, Wendy," Lockjaw said.

Wendy dug him harder and suddenly Kickapoo took off. He galloped halfway to the opposite fence before Wendy reined him in. "What's your problem anyway?" she said. Gaining control, she turned him and they trotted back to Lockjaw.

"Guess he figgered one lesson was enough for today."

"Well, he figured wrong," Wendy said. She jerked him around to the barrel again, but he refused to take the right lead. She backed off again and again, urging his right lead.

"Don't lose your patience," Lockjaw said. "Take your time."

That's easy to say, Wendy thought, feeling hot and cross as the sun warmed the pasture. Sweat trickled down the sides of her face. Her neck and back felt wet. She tugged at Kickapoo's reins, squeezed her legs against his heaving sides and willed him around the barrels several more times. After awhile, she was aware of a different voice calling to her, but she paid little attention, until the voice insisted.

"Wendy Herstead, come here this minute."

Wendy glanced up and saw Mom standing alongside Lockjaw, with her hands on her hips. That usually meant trouble, so she trotted over in a hurry.

"You should have been here the first time Kickapoo went around the barrels, Mom," Wendy began. "He really liked it."

"That's fine," Mom said in a flat voice. "But what about the chickens? Did you feed them this morning? Did you gather the eggs? Have you started watering the garden yet? It's going to be hot as all get out today and you can't water the garden once the sun is high."

"I'm going to, Mom. I've just got to make Kickapoo do this right one more time."

"And you can't take up Lockjaw's time with this nonsense either," Mom went on. "He's got plenty to do without you bothering him."

"But, Mom. . . ."

"No more 'but Moms,'" she said. "You made an agreement, Wendy, and you're going to stick to it."

Wendy glanced at Lockjaw out of the corner of her eye. He was looking down, hands stuffed deep in his pockets, as he studied the ground. Had she gotten him in trouble too, she wondered. Probably, the way Mom sounded. Wendy turned Kickapoo around and headed for the barn, feeling discouraged and upset over the turn the morning had taken. After such a good beginning, too, she thought. Well, she decided, things can only get better tomorrow.

Spoon Money

Wendy waved to Mom through the window of the station wagon, then relaxed on the back seat between Beaver and Kim as the car moved down the lane. Janet sat in front with her Mom. Mrs. Marshall had volunteered to do the driving each week because dancing class came on the same day as her hairdresser's appointment. Now she reached for the air conditioning button and almost immediately, cool air wafted through the car.

Oh neat, Wendy thought, feeling her stickiness evaporate. She'd been waiting for Mrs. Marshall in the yard, and getting hotter by the second in this silly dress Mom had made her wear. A pair of shorts and a halter top would have been a lot cooler, but Mom said you didn't wear that sort of thing to dancing class.

"Is this your third lesson, Wendy?" Mrs. Marshall asked her pleasantly.

"Yes, m'am. I started a week later than everybody else."

"But you should see her, Mom," Janet said. "She can really dance."

"Yeah," Beaver said. "And she doesn't step on my toes like the heavyweight I had to dance with last week."

"Now Beaver," Mrs. Marshall began. "It takes some people longer than others."

"Yes, ma'am." Beaver rolled his eyes in a long-suffering look.

"I wish we'd do some modern stuff pretty soon," Kim said. "I'm tired of that old fox trot we've been doing. It's so weird."

"It's more like the *ox* trot when the heavyweight does it," Beaver said. Then he collapsed in laughter at his own joke.

Wendy listened for a moment as Mrs. Marshall scolded Beaver, then tuned everybody out. She had important plans to think about for the spoons from her collection that she'd hidden in her purse.

Somehow, today, Wendy was going to leave dancing class and see about selling them. It couldn't be done on Saturdays when she came to town with Mom. That was too risky. And now she just couldn't wait any longer. She'd put it off for a couple of weeks because she felt so awful about the whole business, especially telling Mom the lie. During those two weeks she'd hoped for some miraculous thing to happen, like finding money in her sock drawer or receiving a letter that said, "Dear Contestant, you have won. . . ."

But nothing did happen, and today the emergency plan must be put into action. The money for the entry fee was due this Saturday. Besides, Kickapoo needed vitamins or extra feed or something, to put a little fire in him and make him turn the barrels better than he was doing. She couldn't ask Mom to pay for anything connected with the rodeo.

Wendy's mind wasn't on dancing today, and she could hardly wait for the ten-minute break in the middle of class. When it finally came, she hurried to the rest room and pulled a piece of paper from her purse. It was a list of store names she'd copied from the phone book last night. Now she studied the addresses carefully. The antique shop was too far to reach from here, but the address of Maude's Bric-a-Brac Shoppe sounded as if it was just around the corner. She'd try that one first, as soon as class started again. If Maude wasn't interested, then she'd try Sam's Secondhand Store across from the post office.

Wendy remained in the lounge, sitting in one of the scratchy wicker chairs and listening to the wheezy sound of Mrs. Twillabee's record player. Just one more minute and it would be safe to go, she thought. Mrs. Twillabee took attendance at the beginning of each class, and never seemed to know one girl from another during class.

The rest room door opened abruptly.

"Wendy," Kim said. "What's the matter?"

"I've got a stomach-ache," Wendy said. She wasn't telling a story; her stomach was churning nervously.

"That's too bad." Kim's reply was vague as she looked at herself in the mirror over the wash basins. After carefully patting her hair, she seemed satisfied and headed for the door. "I'll tell Mrs. Twillabee," she said and was gone.

Wendy followed her out, then tiptoed behind the plastic ferns and palms to the door that led downstairs. She could hear the shuffling and scraping of feet from the ballroom, and Mrs. Twillabee's voice calling out the time as she clapped her hands together in rhythm. No one seemed to have noticed Wendy's absence.

Wendy carefully opened the stairway door, feeling a sudden blast of hot air engulf her as she stepped from the cool hall. Then she quickly ran down the steps and almost knocked Beaver flat as they collided in the doorway.

"Where you going?" he asked, his jaws working on a large, gooey lump in his mouth.

"Are you chewing gum?" Wendy asked, hoping to divert him. "You know you're not supposed to chew gum when you're wearing braces."

"Who cares?" he said as she tried to push by him. "Where you headed? Class isn't over yet, is it?"

"No, and you'd better get up there fast before Mrs. Twillabee finds out you've sneaked down to the drugstore to buy gum."

"I hope she does," he said, shifting the lump from one side to the other. "Then maybe she'll fire me from dancing class." He fell in beside Wendy as she started down Main Street. "Where are we going?"

Wendy knew he wouldn't be easy to shake. "Beaver," she began, her voice loud and unnatural. "Beaver, promise me you'll never breathe a word."

"I promise," Beaver said, nearly swallowing his gum. "What did you do?"

"I haven't done anything," Wendy answered. "It's just that, well, I have a business problem."

"Huh?" Beaver's eyes squinted skeptically. "What kind of business problem?"

"Oh, never mind. Someday, when you're older, you'll understand."

"Just exactly how old are you?" he asked.

Wendy ignored him, wishing the sidewalk would swallow him up. For a moment she thought she'd really lost him when Beaver stopped to admire pyramids of sweet rolls and doughnuts in the bakery shop window. Then he caught up to her as she turned off Main and onto Green. There, just ahead, was the sign, Maude's Bric-a-Brac Shoppe. Wendy felt clammy cold with fright now. Talking to strangers had always been difficult for her. This was even worse.

The doorbell tinkled lightly as Wendy and Beaver entered. Wendy looked around at the gaudy trinkets on display and wished the pounding in her head would stop. Then a woman in a brightly colored skirt appeared from the back room. Her yellow hair lay in sausage shapes around her head.

"Yes, dear, you want to buy a present for your mother?" she asked.

Wendy drew a deep breath and swallowed hard. "No, ma'am. I wonder, that is, well, I've got some spoons to sell." The tight collar on her dress seemed to be choking her.

The woman raised an eyebrow. "You want to sell

me something? This isn't a hock shop, young lady."

"Yes, ma'am, I know." Wendy had a terrible headache now. "But I've got these spoons. . . ."

"If you've stolen something, you ought to be reported to the police."

"I *didn't* steal anything!" Wendy found herself shouting. "They're *my* spoons and I can do what I like with them!" She turned and ran from the store.

"Wendy, wait," Beaver called. They hurried down the street. "Hey, what's going on? Why do you need to sell your spoons?"

Wendy was so upset she spilled out her troubles, glad to confide in someone at last.

"I wish I could help," Beaver said, as they headed for Sam's Secondhand Store.

They entered the musty old shop and Sam appeared from the back of the store. Wendy couldn't look away from his wrinkled old face. His eyes, Wendy thought. They look like melted chocolate; and they're the kindest eyes I've ever seen.

"Sam!" Beaver said. "I didn't know you were *this* Sam."

"Beaver," the old man spoke softly. "How's my old friend?"

Wendy listened to them for a moment, then Beaver stopped to explain. "Sam's my best fishing friend in the whole world," he said. "He comes out to the pond every summer and we have a contest to see who can catch the biggest fish."

"What brings you here, Beaver?" Sam asked.

Quickly Beaver explained Wendy's problem. "I think we can arrange something," Sam said, looking at the ten spoons Wendy now showed him.

Beaver and Wendy left a few minutes later, with a promise from Sam to buy the remaining eleven spoons still at home.

"I'll try my best not to sell your spoons, Wendy," Sam said as they left. "I'll give you every chance to buy them back."

Tears of gratitude flooded Wendy's eyes as they hurried down the street. She hoped she wouldn't do something awful now like cry in front of the other kids. Fiercely she wiped her cheeks. Then they ran up the stairs to Mrs. Twillabee's and opened the door just in time to hear class being dismissed.

Later, driving home in the car, Mrs. Marshall said, "What's the matter with everyone? Beaver, you're unusually quiet. Anything wrong?"

He shook his head and looked out the window. Mrs. Marshall glanced at him in the rear-view mirror.

"What's the matter, Beaver?" Wendy whispered.

He opened his mouth and displayed shards of gum clinging to his braces. The gum looked like rubber bands going in every direction, threatening to snap his teeth together in a sticky, gluey grip.

Wendy didn't want to laugh, but she couldn't help it. If she didn't laugh, she knew she'd cry and she really wasn't certain just which she felt like doing anyway. She laughed until her stomach ached and tears flooded her eyes. How can I want to laugh and cry at the same time, she wondered. Will there ever be a time this summer when I understand how I feel about anything?

A Nightmare

After counting the spoon money once again, Wendy put it back in an envelope and tucked it away in her desk drawer. She sighed, still hurting over the loss of her spoons. Would Sam be forced to sell them, she wondered. She wouldn't blame him if he did. After all, they were his, now, until she could buy them back.

She turned off the bedside lamp and opened the window as wide as it would go. She climbed onto the bed and pulled the sheet over her, but soon kicked it off. The air was hot and still. It had to rain soon.

Wendy clasped her hands behind her head and turned to the window, hoping for a cool breath of air. Slowly her mind slipped back to her money problems. She had nineteen dollars left, which would just barely cover the hauling fee and, maybe, a new pair of jeans for the rodeo. There was no way she could afford a new western shirt and hat now. Then what shirt would she wear? It was supposed to be bright and colorful, according to the regulations. Barrel race girls add color to the rodeos, not only with their riding but with their bright gay clothing. At least that's what it said in the handbooks. Now what did she have that was bright and gay? Not her faded red shirt; it looked old even from a distance. Mentally she ticked off the rest of the blouses in her closet, but nothing fit the handbook description. Well, she thought, if Kickapoo doesn't start performing better, I won't have to worry about being bright and gay in the arena. Only two weeks to go, she thought in sudden panic. Only two weeks to go!

She sat up suddenly, hugging her knees to her chest. Now why did she have to think about that tonight? She didn't want to, but there it was, boiling up to the top of her mind. Somehow, all her thoughts these days circled around Kick's lack of cooperation. Oh, he would trot, even gallop up to the oil drums, then maybe turn one before refusing to try the others.

Like that scene late this afternoon . . . .

Wendy waited until she'd fed the chickens and the

temperature had cooled down before she worked Kickapoo. First, they had gone for a nice easy lope around the pasture. Kickapoo liked to loosen his legs this way and Wendy enjoyed the close feeling she had with him. Gradually, Wendy urged him into a gallop for one final stretch before they started on the barrels. Oh, what a stride he had, Wendy thought. Kickapoo had to be one of the most pleasurable horses around to ride. People told her so, people who really knew. He was a great pleasure horse. Then why, she asked herself as they halted near the barrels, why couldn't he barrel race too?

She let him cool down a minute or two before easing him into the pattern. They took the first barrel in a comfortable lope, Kick using his right lead beautifully. Then she urged him to the second barrel and he took the circle fast and easy there too. He seemed almost eager to do it after he switched to his left lead. Good. So far better than good. Great. Then they headed for the final barrel at the top of the triangle. Suddenly he balked and kicked over the barrel. Wendy lost her stirrup. She groped for it as Kickapoo shied and tried to bolt.

"Kickapoo," she shouted. "Whoa."

She pulled him up short, and retrieved her stirrup. Then Wendy reached over to stroke his neck.

55

"Come on," she said. "Don't panic. It's okay." She talked to him in a soothing tone now and his ears switched back and forth as if he wanted to catch every syllable. After a moment, Wendy turned in the saddle to see Lockjaw standing by the fence. They ambled over to him.

"Maybe the training is too fast," Lockjaw said. "After all, the pros take a long time to season a barrel horse."

"But the other kids can get their horses to work," Wendy said. "I know because I've seen them. And it's not as if Kickapoo and I have just met. Besides, he knows very well what I've got in mind."

"Some horses have a lot more try than others," Lockjaw reminded her.

Wendy knew what he meant. Some horses were born to do anything. Just squeeze their girth a little, lead with the reins slightly, talk to them gently and they could probably do the fox trot at Mrs. Twillabee's.

Buckwheat strolled along the fence to them. She nudged Lockjaw's arm as if to remind him she needed a friendly scratch on the nose. Lockjaw obliged.

"You're a nice old gal," he said. "But good for absolutely nothin'."

"I wonder what it would be like to ride her," Wendy said.

"She's still got plenty of miles in her," Lockjaw said. "I imagine she'd get you where you wanted to go."

"Let's see what happens," Wendy said. She dropped down from Kick's back and hopped on Buckwheat. The Palomino looked up, startled at first, then turned away from Lockjaw's scratching.

"Come on Buckwheat, give me a bareback ride," Wendy said, holding onto her mane.

Slowly Buckwheat gathered herself into a lope along the pasture fence. They followed it down to the corner and stopped under an old chinaberry tree.

"Okay, Buckwheat, take me home," Wendy urged. She kicked her slightly with the heels of her boots and that seemed to be the only prodding the old horse needed. She turned around and stretched out into a gallop that made Wendy braid her fingers into the horse's mane in a fierce grip. Buckwheat ran up to Kickapoo and Lockjaw by the fence, and stopped easily in the middle of a pivot.

"Wow," Wendy said breathlessly. "She's fast. I wonder what she was like when she was younger."

Wendy sighed now as she remembered this afternoon. Then she fluffed her pillow on one side and turned over. Sure, Buckwheat was fast, but Kickapoo was quicker and once he'd caught onto barrel racing, he'd be unbeatable in every department. I know it, she thought. I just know it.

Despite her knotted-up feeling about Kickapoo, Wendy soon fell asleep. She had worked in the garden for the better part of the day, and tonight she was bone-tired. Now her dreams involved the long rows of beans she'd been hoeing this afternoon. They stretched as far as she could see, to the farthest horizon of her dream. There, at the end of the rows, stood Kickapoo, waiting for her . . . .

Something awakened her suddenly. Wendy wasn't sure what it was at first, then realized that she felt prickly cold all over. Her curtains flapped in a cool night breeze. Quickly she got up and pulled the window partway down, just in case of rain. She was about to scurry back to bed when she noticed an unfamiliar car parked in the driveway. A rectangle of light from the living-room window cast its reflection on the yard directly below.

"I wonder what's going on," she mumbled sleepily, holding her alarm clock close to see what time it was. The hands pointed to 12:45.

Wendy climbed back in bed and pulled the sheet and a lightweight blanket over her. She turned several times, trying to find a comfortable position. Who would stay here until nearly one o'clock in the morning, she thought, remembering now that Mom hadn't mentioned company coming.

Then Wendy grinned. Maybe Mom has a boyfriend and doesn't want me to know, she thought. The more she considered that, the wider awake she became. Suddenly Wendy sat up. What if Mom got married again? How would their lives change? Would she like him? Wendy had never thought about someone replacing Dad until now, but Mom was still young and pretty. Why shouldn't she get married again?

Now Wendy could hear voices in the living room. Quietly she got out of bed and opened the door. This wasn't eavesdropping exactly. She just wanted to know what was going on.

She tiptoed to the top of the stairs and sat down to listen. The voices were so low she couldn't hear them distinctly at first, then she realized she was hearing only women's voices. Mom's voice, and the other voice belonged to — why it was Aunt Sally! She was about to rush down the stairs when she overheard Aunt Sally's next remark.

"Stop putting me on a pedestal for Wendy to copy. It isn't fair to her and it isn't fair to me."

"Shhhh," Mom's voice hushed her. "You'll wake her up."

"Maybe we ought to," Aunt Sally continued, but more quietly than before. "Maybe she ought to hear that I cut my trip short because I was so bored with it."

I've never heard Aunt Sally talk like this before, Wendy thought. She's usually so happy all the time. What does she mean about being up on a pedestal for me to copy?

"I didn't know you felt this way," Mom was saying. "Your life always seemed so perfect to me."

"I know you believed that, Helen," Aunt Sally said. "But even if it were true, it's not fair to Wendy to insist that she become like me. You can't change a person into someone she doesn't want to be or can't become. We all deserve the right to be ourselves."

Oh thank you, Aunt Sally, Wendy thought. Now, maybe, Mom will forget all about the fancy dresses and dancing lessons and let me barrel race as much as I want to.

There was a long silence as Wendy waited for Mom's answer. Would she say that she understood at last?

Finally, she couldn't wait any longer. Wendy stood up, prepared to dash down the stairs when Aunt Sally broke the silence. "Oh, by the way, Helen. I bought something for Wendy in Hong Kong. You'll love it too, I think."

"What is it?" Mom's voice sounded far away.

"It's a beautiful teakwood display case for Wendy's spoons."

Wendy's stomach lurched sickeningly as she made her way back to her bedroom and quietly closed the door. She dreaded tomorrow, knowing that she'd have to tell them what she had done with the spoons.

Wendy's Desperate Decision

"Wendy, how could you?" Mom said. "How could you sell your spoons?"

Wendy stared at her scrambled eggs and shook her head. She didn't look at Aunt Sally and Mom who were seated at the kitchen table with her. All she could do was stare miserably at her plate and wish for a miracle to happen, like an earthquake that would swallow her up and make her disappear forever.

The teakwood display case sat on the table where Lockjaw's plate normally would be. He had eaten long ago and left for the fields. Eating later when Aunt Sally came to visit had always been a treat for Wendy, but not this morning. She had wakened earlier than usual, after tossing most of the night in dread of the scene now taking place.

"But why?" Mom was saying. "Why did you lie to me?"

"Helen," Aunt Sally put in. She spread her long thin fingers on the plastic tablecloth. Her bright red nails clashed with the orange squares. "It's none of my business, but she's having a pretty rough time of it. . . ."

"Sally," Mom's voice was firm. "She told me a lie and I think I need — deserve — to know the reason."

"Of course," Sally said. "Meantime, I'll retrieve the spoons. I'll go down to the store where she sold them and buy them back."

"No." Mom said it at the same instant that Wendy did. She was startled as they looked at one another, to realize they were in agreement over this point, anyway.

"No," Mom said again. "That's too easy. Wendy won't learn anything from that."

"Thank you, Aunt Sally." Wendy found her voice at last, but it sounded rusty as if she hadn't used it for a long time. "Thank you, but no."

The telephone rang and Mom walked across the kitchen to answer it.

"Why didn't you let me know?" Aunt Sally asked.

She shook her blonde hair away from her face. "You know I would have sent you the money for the rodeo."

"I know, Aunt Sally," Wendy said. "But I made an agreement with Mom that I would pay for it. Besides, I wanted to do it all by myself. Except . . ." her voice broke as she continued. "I just hated selling my spoons."

Mom put the telephone receiver back in the cradle, and picked up the coffee pot from the stove to pour a second cup for Aunt Sally and herself. Wendy pushed her untouched plate of scrambled eggs away from her.

"Well," Aunt Sally said. She tried to keep her voice light. "This isn't the end of the world you know. That display case can be used for lots of other things."

"Oh, Sally." Mom shook her head and stirred her coffee hard. After a moment Aunt Sally stood up and gathered her light blue robe closer to her.

"I think I'll take my bath now," she said. "Excuse me." Mom and Wendy waited to speak until she left.

"Wendy," Mom said. "I've been against the rodeo from the start. I made no secret of it, did I?"

"No."

"But I finally decided that if you took over the

responsibility of paying your own expenses, then you could go ahead, at least this one time. Under any other circumstances, you could still take part in the rodeo."

Wendy felt her breath nearly freeze in her throat. Oh, no, she thought. Don't say it, please don't.

"But you lied to me. Told me you had money that you didn't have. Then you sold your beautiful spoons and tried to keep that from me too."

"Mom, I know what I did, and I promise that I'll never lie to you again. You and I know it's the only one I've ever told. But the spoons belonged to me. They were mine to sell if I wanted to, weren't they?"

Yes," her mother said, after a moment's hesitation. "I guess that's right. But the lie still stands. I won't sign the medical release for the rodeo."

"Mom, please don't keep me out of the barrel race. Please."

"Wendy, we aren't going to talk about it any more. I've made my decision."

"Mom, please. . . ."

"Wendy, the subject is closed." Her mother picked up some dishes and carried them over to the sink.

Wendy fought to control the sobs which rattled

inside her. "Mom, haven't you ever wanted anything this much?"

Mom turned and looked at her.

"Isn't there anything in the world that you ever wanted to do as much as this?" Wendy repeated. She felt the tears streaming down her cheeks as she spoke.

Mom looked as if she were about to say something, then abruptly turned back to the sink and the dishes.

Wendy ran from the kitchen and upstairs to her bedroom, slamming the door behind her. Throwing herself on the bed, she cried until her pillow was wet. When she finally ran out of tears, anger and resentment welled up inside, almost choking her.

It's not fair, she thought, walking around her room. Mom's using this one little lie to keep me out of the rodeo. But was she completely honest with *me*? She didn't tell me about being a barrel racer. I had to find that out from Janet.

It's just not fair, she thought again, and kicked the chair in front of her desk.

"Ouch," she said and limped over to her pile of clothes.

She slipped into jeans and a blouse, wondering what to do for the rest of the day. The garden didn't need her and even if it did, she wouldn't work in it.

No way. Lying across her rumpled bed, Wendy let all her bad feelings come to the surface. How could she ever like Mom after this? She'd never understand her again, never in a million years.

Wendy heard a horse galloping up the lane and looked out the window. She saw Janet on Hoofer, and remembered that they'd planned to practice the barrels this morning. What was the point of it now, Wendy thought. Disappointment was like a bad taste in her mouth.

"Hi, Janet." She tried to sound normal as she waved from her window. "Be right down."

Janet dismounted and led Hoofer toward the pasture gate. Wendy joined them there.

"I'm getting so excited, aren't you?" Janet began. "Less than two weeks now until the rodeo. It's going to be so neat, riding in the opening ceremonies with the flags and all."

"Yeah," Wendy mumbled. She hurried ahead to busy herself with opening the gate.

"I just wish we didn't have to wait so long for the barrel race event," Janet continued. "It's nearly always in the second half of the rodeo, after intermission."

"Uhmmm."

"I'm afraid I'll get so nervous, I'll fall off Hoofer,"

Janet laughed. She brushed her short brown hair away from her forehead.

"I'll be right back," Wendy said. "I need to get my tack." She hurried toward the barn while Janet mounted Hoofer and began to warm up. A plan had begun to shape itself in Wendy's mind. She decided she wouldn't say anything about not being in the rodeo to her friend right now. First of all, it was just too grim to talk about. Besides, if she carried out her new plan, she'd be in it after all. Determination set her mouth in a straight line as she lugged her saddle back to the pasture. I'm going to barrel race on Kickapoo, she thought. Nobody can keep me from it.

Wendy saw Janet on Hoofer running alongside the fence, with Buckwheat trailing after them.

"What's the matter with old Buckwheat?" Janet asked, watching Wendy as she saddled Kickapoo. "She must be feeling good this morning."

"She's like that most of the time," Wendy said. "I think she likes company and just follows along. Once in awhile she's a pest, though, and gets in the way."

Janet guided Hoofer to the barrels and walked him through the clover leaf pattern. He takes the turns nice and easy, Wendy thought, as she walked Kickapoo, then loped him up and down the fence. When she felt he was warmed up, they returned to the barrels and she set him in the pattern behind Hoofer. He walked through easily enough; she didn't have to worry about his leads in the walk. It was only when she urged him into a lope or gallop, she thought, that he started balking.

Soon Janet picked up the pace and loped Hoofer through the routine. The Appaloosa followed instructions perfectly. Then Janet gave him a break and paused to watch Wendy. Wendy felt a little self-conscious now, knowing her friend's expert eyes were on her. Sure enough, on the last barrel, Kickapoo shied away and lost his rhythm.

"Kickapoo, you're going to be a barrel horse or my name isn't Wendy Herstead," she shouted angrily. Wendy knew instantly that she shouldn't have blown up like that but her desolate feeling of disappointment and lack of sleep had worn down her control.

"Hey, Wendy," Janet rode up. "Maybe you ought to work on changing leads some more. Seems like Kickapoo needs . . ."

"You don't have to tell me what he needs," Wendy said, spitting the words out. "I know what he needs. He needs to know I'm boss."

"Well, if you're going to be so nasty, I'm going

home," Janet said. She turned Hoofer around and headed for the gate. Wendy rode after her.

"Janet," Wendy called. "Wait a minute."

Janet halted Hoofer and turned around in her saddle.

"I'm sorry," Wendy said. "I didn't want to say that, it just came out. I didn't mean to be so rotten."

"That's all right," Janet said. "I shouldn't have gotten mad. I'm sorry, too." They returned to the barrels and Buckwheat hurried up to them.

"Good old Bucky," Janet said, reaching over to pat her neck. "She sure acts like the world's her best friend, doesn't she?"

"Yes," Wendy said. "She does."

"Wendy," Janet hesitated. "You and I . . . we're best friends, aren't we?"

"Sure, of course we are."

"So if you've got a problem, you know, something on your mind, you can tell me, can't you? I mean, best friends tell best friends everything."

Wendy looked at Janet and wanted to tell it all. But she couldn't yet. "I'll tell you soon, Janet. Real soon."

"Okay."

"Let's go for a ride. I don't want to practice any more right now."

"Okay."

They headed for the opposite pasture gate, with Buckwheat running alongside. Wendy needed to keep ahead of Janet so she couldn't see the tears that were threatening again. She had to keep moving or she'd blurt out everything about her new plan. Wendy had just decided she was going to run away.

"They Never Forget"

In the two days since Mom had found out about the spoons, there'd been an uneasy truce between them. Neither Wendy nor Mom spoke directly to one another, but each seemed to be watching the other, waiting for a word or look that said they could start negotiations again. Meanwhile, Aunt Sally was trying to carry on as if everything were okay. She talked too loud at mealtimes, told jokes that weren't funny, and made a mess of any work she tried to do.

"Look, Wendy," she said this morning as they gathered eggs together. "You and your Mom have to talk pretty soon. This silent treatment is driving me crazy."

"I said I was sorry for telling the lie," Wendy replied. "I said I'd never tell another one. And I mean it."

"Do you want me to talk to her?" Aunt Sally asked, dropping an egg in the basket so hard that the shell cracked. "There's still time for you to be in the rodeo."

"It's no use." Wendy's voice was flat and dull. "She won't change her mind."

After supper, Wendy excused herself early. She went up to her room, closed the door and locked it, then began her preparations to leave. A suitcase would be unmanageable on Kickapoo so she placed the things she'd need on an old blanket. Wendy tossed in an extra pair of jeans, two shirts, some underwear, and toilet articles. The rodeo papers went in an envelope with her money. Then she rolled everything into the blanket and tied it on the ends with an old jump rope. She pushed the blanket roll under the bed, undressed partway, unlocked the door and hopped in bed to wait until it was time to leave. Soon she heard a knock.

"Come in."

"Wendy, are you awake?" It was Mom. Maybe...

"Yes."

"Can we talk?"

"Sure."

"I just wanted to say that someday you'd understand how I feel about all this." Mom sat on the edge of the bed.

"I don't think so."

"Wendy, the lessons we have to learn as we're growing up are hard to take sometimes."

Wendy heard Mom's words but rejected them. Right now, she rejected everything about Mom. Her words, her authority, even her perfume. "I looked at your rodeo scrapbooks, Mom."

"Did you?"

"I don't think anything could have kept you from barrel racing either." Wendy turned over so that she faced the wall now. "Goodnight, Mom."

She heard Mom sigh. "Goodnight, Wendy." The door closed behind her.

Wendy sat up and listened. Then she moved to the window and looked out. The night was freshly washed with moonlight and Wendy was glad for that. Running away was scary enough. If it had been pitch black, she'd be shaking in her boots. Maybe she wouldn't even have the courage to try it. Then she thought of Kickapoo and the rodeo. I'll do it, she thought. I'm going to barrel race.

She waited forever, it seemed, until no reflection of light came from the downstairs windows. Now the house was quiet and seemed to breathe on its own. It was time. Wendy picked up her blanket roll, boots, and jacket, and slipped quietly out and headed for the barn. She'd had a tough time explaining to Lockjaw earlier this evening why she chose to put Kick in a stall rather than leave him in pasture. But she had to lessen the chances of someone seeing and hearing her saddle him now. As Wendy put on her boots, Hector came to rub against he.

"Hello, you old chicken thief," she said, stroking him. "Take care of those hens while I'm gone." Suddenly it all sounded so real and so final that tears clouded Wendy's vision. When would she be home? Not until after the rodeo, if then. Maybe Mom wouldn't want her back . . . .

She turned without daring to finish the thought and began to saddle Kickapoo. He seemed undisturbed, as if going for moonlight walks were a common event. Wendy bent over to check the cinch belt once more and found herself staring at a pair of boots that didn't belong to her. Startled, she jumped nervously and looked up into Lockjaw's face.

"Beautiful night for a ride," he said softly.

"Don't try to stop me." Wendy sounded stern. "I'm not going to stay here any longer."

"Okay." He sounded as if it were all the same to him. "Where are you going?"

She looked at him, ready to explode.

"I just want to know where to send your mail," he said.

"Lockjaw." She tried to stay mad. Mad at him, mad at Mom, mad at the world. But the truth was, she didn't know where she was going, didn't have a place to go. "Oh, Lockjaw." She hugged Kickapoo and tried to hold back her feelings, but it was so useless.

"Come on, little railbird," Lockjaw said, taking the reins from her. "Let's pull up a bale of hay and talk things over."

They sat down outside the stall as Kickapoo watched them curiously. In the bright moonlight, Wendy could see Lockjaw's face, worry lines crisscrossing it like a road map.

"Now, what's ailin' you?"

Wendy spilled it all out, about the money, the spoons, and how Mom was using her misbehavior as an excuse to keep her out of the rodeo. But she was going to be in it, riding Kickapoo, no matter what. So there.

"Mom wants me to grow up to be like Aunt Sally, but it just isn't in me," she finished. "She's trying to make me something I'm not."

"But you shouldn't be mad at your Mom, Wendy,"

Lockjaw said. "You should try to understand."

"I'll never understand, Lockjaw. I'll never understand Mom at all."

Hector braided himself around Lockjaw's legs and began to purr.

"And now you're planning to ride Kickapoo in the barrel race, anyway?" His abrupt change of subject puzzled Wendy.

"You know I am."

"Even if he's not a barrel horse and never will be?"

"But he is," Wendy insisted. "You'll see. Even if it isn't in him, I'll make him become a barrel horse."

"Hector," Lockjaw scratched the cat's battered ears. "You're the lucky one. You get to be yourself, just a ragged old chicken chaser. Nobody's trying to change you into something you're not."

Wendy stared at Lockjaw, his words echoing in her head. Good grief, she thought. What's my problem? I've been trying to change Kickapoo in the same way that Mom has been trying to change me. I love him so much that I haven't been able to see him as he really is.

She entered Kickapoo's stall now and hugged him fiercely. Then she stood back and looked at him, as if she were seeing him for the first time. He was a beautiful sorrel gelding who liked to amble through life at his own pace. He wasn't an athlete and he had no try, but he was still the best pleasure horse around, she thought loyally. The very best.

She accepted Kickapoo now for what he was, and slowly all the anger and resentment she felt toward her mother melted away. I understand, Wendy thought. Just like she said. Understanding seemed more important than anything else now, even more important than the rodeo. Wendy suddenly felt at peace with herself and all the feelings about Mom that had mixed her up this summer.

Mom loves me, she thought. Mom really loves me, maybe even more than I love Kickapoo.

And then she heard it, a funny, tinny sound coming from a long way away. At first she thought it was Lockjaw still sitting outside the stall, drumming on something with his fingers. Then he stood up to look in at her with a puzzled expression on his face.

"What was that?" she felt the need to whisper.

"Don't know exactly. Listen." They heard it again, coupled now with a rhythmic thudding sound.

"Like somebody playing kick the can," she said.

More tinny sounds cluttered the still night air. They closed Kickapoo's stall and hurried to the door.

"Sounds like it's coming from the pasture," Wendy said. "Hurry, Lockjaw." They ran out of the barn and down the hill. In the moonlight, the trees created free-form shadows on the ground. The house was a large dark block against the light sky. Now one rectangle of light appeared in the block, her mother's room. Then another, her own room, then another, Aunt Sally's room.

Wendy stopped at the rise overlooking the pasture. Lockjaw hurried up, puffing slightly.

"Look," she said quietly. "Look at Buckwheat."

They watched together while the old Palomino ran the cloverleaf pattern around the barrels, taking them in tight, neat turns. She ran in perfect rhythm and balance, tossing her mane occasionally as if responding to unheard applause. Now and again, as she turned the barrels, she nicked them with one of her shoes and the funny, tinny sound echoed back to them. In the moonlight, the Palomino looked like a spirited ghost horse to Wendy, running a pattern she'd learned from a long time ago. Now she pranced and pivoted to unseen signals, then returned to a starting gate that only she knew about.

"Doc never told me she was a barrel horse," Lockjaw said. "His daughter musta rode her." His voice sounded reverent, as if he were in church.

"Bucky must have been the best," Wendy breathed. "I think she still is."

Mom and Aunt Sally appeared by the pasture gate to watch, and now Wendy and Lockjaw hurried down to join them.

"They never forget," Mom said, tears glittering in her eyes as she watched Buckwheat. Then she put her arms around Wendy and hugged her tightly. "But I almost did," she whispered. "I almost forgot what it's like to be twelve and want something so much."

"Oh, Mom, do you mean . . . ."

"I mean, if you work very hard, there's still time for you and Buckwheat to get ready for the rodeo."

The Great Day

It's rodeo day, Wendy thought, without opening her eyes. She stretched lazily in bed, enjoying the feeling that the special day had at last arrived. Opening her eyes now, she looked to the window and saw bright sun streaming through the curtains that swayed in a slight breeze. A perfect day, and definitely rodeo day.

Quickly she dressed and ran downstairs. There was so much to do. Automatically she grabbed the egg basket on the back porch, but it wasn't there. While she stood looking for it, the hens began a staccato cackling.

If Hector has everybody riled up today, Wendy thought, running for the henhouse, I'll lock him in the barn for the rest of the summer. She closed the gate behind her and turned to see Aunt Sally emerge from the henhouse, smiling happily.

"Surprise," she said, holding the egg basket high. "Thought I'd do your chores today." Wendy smiled her thanks. Aunt Sally really had started helping this last week. She pulled weeds and fed chickens and scrubbed milk cans almost like a pro, and didn't seem to mind that she'd broken all her long fingernails.

Together now they scattered corn and filled water cans. As they watched the hens and roosters scratch at their food, Aunt Sally said, "Nervous?"

"Just a little," Wendy admitted. "More excited than anything else."

"That's natural," Aunt Sally said. "I'm a little nervous myself."

They hurried to the kitchen where Mom was flipping pancakes and Lockjaw stood washing his hands at the sink. No one said much during the meal, but Wendy could feel all their thoughts mingling together, bent on the event this afternoon. Breakfast over, Aunt Sally quickly began clearing the table.

"Wendy, come upstairs a minute," Mom said. "I want to show you something."

Wendy hurried after Mom. A box lay on her bed and now Mom opened it. "This was my barrel race outfit when I rode," Mom began. "I know the pants are too big for you, but you could wear the shirt if we take a couple of tucks. That is, if you want to."

Wendy picked up the shirt and held it next her. It was a bright Kelly green with lots of small spangly mirrors sewn on it. When she shook the blouse slightly, all the little mirrors caught the sun and reflected off the walls.

"Oh, Mom, it's beautiful," Wendy said. Quickly she put it on and Mom got busy with pins, shaping it to Wendy's slight frame.

"This won't take long." Mom talked through pins in her mouth.

Wendy changed back into her old shirt and ran from the room, out of the house, and down to the pasture. Quickly she entered and Buckwheat hurried up to her, with Kickapoo following at his own pace.

The past ten days have been just great, riding Buckwheat, she thought. Actually, she had little to do but time her own moves with the mare's. Buckwheat's instincts were so good and she had so much try that she was really teaching Wendy. She never seems to tire either, Wendy thought. Although she was older than Kickapoo, she had stayed in good shape, probably because she made such a pest of herself all summer, and insisted on being part of his training.

Now Wendy patted Buckwheat, then hugged Kickapoo. The day was perfect, or nearly so, Wendy thought. Her dream had been to ride Kick in the rodeo, but now she knew it never could be. Kick had his own ideas, and she was grateful to him for that, really.

At noon, the man who rented horse trailers drove up in his pickup.

"Howdy, Gus." Lockjaw hurried to greet him. Wendy followed from the kitchen.

"I'll get Buckwheat." She ran to the pasture, threw a halter on her, and led the mare to the trailer.

"Hey," Gus said. "That looks like Doc Galloway's horse."

"That's right," Lockjaw said.

"You gonna ride her?" Gus asked Wendy.

"Sure am," she smiled.

Gus kicked a stone. "Well," he said. "Good luck."

Wendy kept smiling as Gus and Lockjaw put Buckwheat in the trailer. She knew Bucky looked like an old nag and more than likely, they wouldn't win. But what did that matter? She was going to barrel race in the rodeo. That was all she really wanted to do.

When Gus handed Wendy the hauling bill, her smile grew. It was less than she'd expected. There was money left over to buy back a couple of spoons this weekend. She counted out her precious dollars in Gus's calloused hand.

"Paid in full." She tapped the last dollar for emphasis.

"It's a pleasure doin' business with you, young lady," he said. Then he climbed in the truck with Lockjaw and they sped off to the rodeo.

Now Wendy hurried. Upstairs she showered and dressed in her rodeo clothes. Her new jeans were a soft yellow, just perfect with Mom's shirt. Someone had tied a green ribbon around her cowboy hat. Was that Aunt Sally's contribution? She looked at herself in the mirror and pulled her long blonde hair down on her shoulders. Should she braid it? No, she decided she'd let it fly free. She was ready.

They drove through Sterling in Aunt Sally's car and headed for the rodeo arena just north of town. Traffic slowed their progress as they neared the entrance, and a policeman halted cars so that Aunt Sally could turn in at the "Contestants" entrance. Wendy smiled as she looked at the sign. That's me, she thought. I'm a contestant in Little Britches rodeo.

They located Buckwheat tied to a fence next to Janet's Hoofer. After Lockjaw, Mom, and Aunt Sally had fussed over her some more, they finally headed for the grandstands.

Wendy looked around for her friends. So many people milled around the trailers and campers now and so many animals stirred up the dust, it was hard to see anyone who looked familiar. She glanced over toward the enclosure that held the bulls, and saw Beaver leaning over the fence. Then she saw Janet hurrying toward her, dressed in a bright-red western outfit.

"Am I glad to see you!" Wendy said. "You look great."

"You too," Janet said. "That shirt is so neat." They turned to saddle their horses. "I'm glad you're going to ride Buckwheat. She'll give you a good ride."

"Hope so." Wendy shortened her stirrups slightly.

They waved to Heidi who was leading her bay gelding toward the arena. Then Kim dashed up in bright blue pants and a checkered shirt.

"Wendy, Janet, isn't it exciting? Just wonderful? What's Buckwheat doing here?" Kim's words tumbled out. "Wendy, look at your shirt. It's got mirrors on it. Hold still." She tried to see herself.

"Oh, Kim, you're crazy," Wendy laughed, as Kim ran off to saddle her horse.

Beaver strolled up now and took off his Stetson and wiped his forehead. "Guess what?" he said, carefully replacing his hat. "I get to carry one of the flags. We're supposed to get in line right now." He hurried away and Janet and Wendy mounted their horses.

"Good luck," Wendy whispered.

"You too," Janet said.

They found their places and rode into the arena as the high school band played a familiar march. Then all the contestants ringed the arena and faced the audience while the colors were posted. The band began to play the national anthem. Wendy felt the afternoon sun on her back and looked up into the bright blue sky. The banners were flying high overhead, and several birds floated in lazy patterns just above her. Oh, she would never forget a minute of this beautiful day. The music ended and Wendy rode out with the other contestants as the announcer droned the names of the officials.

Wendy headed back to the fence and waited. She was too nervous to watch from the contestants' area, but she could tell what was happening from here.

When the calves were moved to the roping chute, she knew calf-roping was next. She listened to the cheers of the audience and the announcer's remarks and hoped that Beaver had won this event. Later, he rode out of the arena, grinning, and flashed an a-okay sign, and she knew that he had.

Intermission came, but Wendy couldn't relax. She watched Heidi eat a cone of cotton candy and felt sick to her stomach. She listened to Beaver tell everyone over and over again, how he had carried a flag and won the calf-roping event. With each telling she grew more fidgety. Finally the announcer said:

"Next event is barrel racing. Will all the contestants get ready?"

Wendy rode up to the group of girls on horses clustered at the arena entrance. Her number was already pinned to her back. She listened as one by one, the girls entered and began their race against time. Then it was Kim's turn. She flashed a big grin and went into the arena with her dark hair flying. Wendy heard the announcer start her off, then a gasp followed from the audience.

"What happened?" Wendy asked Janet, who was next.

"Kim's horse fell."

"Is Kim okay?"

"Yes, she's walking off now. And her horse is up, too."

Wendy breathed a long sigh. What a bad break for Kim. Then it was Janet's turn on Hoofer. The announcer told her to start and Wendy heard the audience cheering as she turned the barrels.

Janet came out, flushed with excitement.

"What was your time?" Wendy asked.

"18.3 seconds," Janet said. "It's the best, so far."

"Great."

"You're next — and last. Good luck," Janet shouted, and Wendy entered the arena.

The crowd clapped, as they did for everyone. Wendy tried to stay calm, but she felt all fluttery inside. She noticed the sandy soil in the arena and suddenly realized how good Janet's time had been.

"We've got our work cut out for us," she whispered and leaned over to pat Buckwheat. Wendy felt the mare's heart beating rapidly against her leg. She was excited too!

"Wendy Herstead, number 42," the announcer called.

Wendy looked at the flagger holding the red flag taut and ready to drop it when she passed him.

"Go," she told herself.

She nudged Buckwheat's sides slightly and they

moved off toward the first barrel, taking it tight but in control. Wendy immediately lined her up with the next barrel and they came in a little fast, nicking it as they turned. Then they headed for the barrel at the top of the triangle and turned it lightly. Buckwheat was giving her finest performance today, and Wendy knew it. She didn't hear the audience urging her on, nor feel the sweat trickling down her face, nor see the clock ticking on the scoreboard. Her total concentration was on Buckwheat. Now they were ready for the final stretch. Wendy grabbed the saddlehorn with her left hand and held the reins lightly in her right. They broke for home in a gallop that was fluid yet powerful, and so fast that Wendy's hat flew off.

"Bring 'er on home, little girl," the announcer called over the loudspeaker. "Bring 'er on home."

A cheer went up as Wendy passed the flagger. Her time flashed on the scoreboard. "Eighteen seconds flat for Wendy Herstead," the announcer shouted. "We have a new winner. Miss Wendy Herstead is Barrel Race Champion of Sterling, Colorado!"

"Congratulations, Wendy," Janet called from behind the fence. Beaver stood on a fence railing and called something to her from cupped hands. Lockjaw appeared behind him, smiling and waving his Stetson.

Wendy waved back to them and to the audience as they continued to clap and cheer. A clown in baggy pants brought her hat to her, bowed low, and fell flat on his face. Then the announcer called:

"Let's clear the arena for the next event."

Wendy heard the horses thrashing in the bucking chute and knew saddle bronc riding was next. As she headed for the gate, a swirl of dust blew in her eyes, and she was glad for the excuse to wipe them. Just before leaving the arena, Wendy turned Buckwheat around and watched as two cowboys rolled the barrels away. Buckwheat nickered and Wendy leaned over to pat her.

"Thanks for the barrel race," she whispered. Slowly Wendy guided Buckwheat out of the arena and through the gate. Then she hurried off to find her friends.